NOW YOU CAN READ....
Cinderella

STORY ADAPTED BY LUCY KINCAID

ILLUSTRATED BY ERIC ROWE

BRIMAX BOOKS • CAMBRIDGE • ENGLAND

Cinderella lived in a big house.
She was ALWAYS busy. Her two
step-sisters made sure of that.
"Cinderella! Sweep the floor!"
"Cinderella! Wash the dishes!"
"Make the beds!"
"Clean the windows!"
Cinderella's work
was NEVER done.

Cinderella's step-sisters spent half the day telling her what to do. They spent the other half trying to look pretty.

"Cinderella! Brush my hair!"

"Cinderella! Tie my bow!"

"Powder my nose!"

"Fasten my buttons!"

One day a letter arrived at the house.

"There is to be a ball at the palace! We are invited!" shouted the step-sisters.

"Am I invited?" asked Cinderella. "Even if you are, you cannot go," said her step-sisters. "You will be too busy getting US ready!"

The day of the ball came. The
step-sisters kept Cinderella VERY
busy indeed. There was SO much
to do. Poor Cinderella did not
know what to do first.

At last, the step-sisters had gone, and the house was quiet. Cinderella sat by the fire and began to cry.

"If only I could have gone to the ball," she wept.

"You shall go to the ball!" said
a voice behind her.
Cinderella jumped up in alarm. She
thought she was alone in the house.
"Who . . . who are you?" she gasped.
"I am your Fairy Godmother," said
the stranger. "I have come to get
YOU ready for the ball."

"Bring me a pumpkin!" said the Fairy Godmother. She turned the pumpkin into a coach.
"Bring me four white mice!" said the Fairy Godmother. She turned the mice into four white horses.

"Bring me three lizards!" said the Fairy Godmother. They became a coach-driver, and two footmen.

"I cannot go to the ball dressed in rags," said Cinderella sadly.

The Fairy Godmother waved her
magic wand once more. Cinderella's
rags turned into a beautiful ball
gown. Her bare feet were covered
with dainty glass slippers.

"Now YOU are ready for the ball,"
said the Fairy Godmother.

"But first, a warning. You must leave before the clock strikes twelve. At twelve everything will change back to the way it was before."

"I will remember," said Cinderella.

"Thank you, dear Fairy Godmother."

Cinderella danced all night with
the Prince. Her step-sisters saw
her, but they did not recognise
her. They thought she was a
visiting princess.

Cinderella was so happy she forgot all about the Fairy Godmother's warning. She did not remember until the palace clock began to strike the chimes of midnight. One . . . two . . . three . . . "I must go!" she cried, and ran from the palace.

"Stop! Stop!"
cried the Prince.
Cinderella did not
hear him.
As she ran down
the palace steps
she lost one of
her glass slippers.

ten . . . eleven . . .
TWELVE!!!!!
The beautiful gown
turned into rags.
The coach turned
into a pumpkin.
The mice and
lizards ran away.

The Prince found her glass slipper lying on the palace steps. He called a footman. "Take this slipper and find its owner. I will marry the girl it fits."

The footman travelled all over the kingdom with the slipper. It fitted no one. At last he came to the house where Cinderella lived. "Let me try it!" said one of her step-sisters. She snatched the slipper from the footman.

"Look!" she cried. "A perfect fit!"

"No it isn't!" shouted the other step-sister. "Your heel is hanging out! Give it to me!" And SHE snatched the glass slipper.

It didn't fit her either. Though she tried to pretend that it did. "Is there anyone else in the house who should try the slipper?" asked the footman.

"NO!" said both step-sisters together.
"Yes there is," said their father. "Cinderella hasn't tried it yet."
"The Prince would never marry HER!" laughed the step-sisters.

"The Prince said EVERYONE must try the slipper," said the footman. It fitted Cinderella perfectly. Her step-sisters were so surprised, they fainted.

The Prince DID marry Cinderella. The step-sisters were at the wedding. They still looked surprised.

All these appear in the pages of the story. Can you find them?

Cinderella

step-sisters

letter

Fairy Godmother